A Curious Garden of Angels

A Curious Garden of Angels

An Exploration from
the Perspective of
a Little White Chicken

Modestly Recorded and Illustrated
from Pearl's Own Words by
J.R. Spiers

GraciePress

Copyright © John Spiers, 2024

First Edition February 2025

ISBN 978-1-7366338-9-2

Published by Gracie Press

GraciePress.com

Dedication

to all those who believe that
Jesus cares about what we care
about including those we love

Chapter 1

At first, the Curious Being that Pearl glimpsed would move from the sunlight and into the shadows and back again. With wings, it appeared to be a bird, but there had never been a bird with feathers colored like those Pearl had seen that morning.

There were feathers that Pearl had seen in the past that reflected light, but the feathers on The Curious Being appeared to actually be radiating light that matched the colors of the camellias and their petals and branches and leaves. If this was so, it was a truly remarkable kind of camouflage.

As a chicken, Pearl was naturally curious and irresistibly drawn to curious things. She felt she simply *had* to study this Curious Being because there might just be a story to tell.

Chapter 2

As The Curious Being moved from the garden shadows and into the sunlight, Pearl was able to get a closer look. What had appeared to be a bird now appeared to be a figure with arms and legs plus wings, but in the sunlight, they didn't appear to be ordinary wings. Instead they were more vibrant and colorful than imaginable.

The Curious Being appeared to have been immersed in the Color of Love, Pearl had only seen this color once before when The Great Gardener's Son had brought two young baby chicks for Pearl to raise as if they were her own.

Pearl knew that anyone who has spent time with Jesus, The Great Gardener's Son, will reflect The Color of Love.

Chapter 3

Whatever this Curious Being was, it had a majesty and a beauty about it like none Pearl had ever seen anywhere. She was mesmerized by the colors she saw on the creatures wings. Pearl decided she needed to talk with The Songbirds of The

Living Library. Pearl was confident that they would have the answers she needed.

The Songbirds of The Living Library have the united purpose of preserving all knowledge since the first birds leaped into the sky and sang out in thanksgiving to The Great Gardener for the gift of flight. They serve answers to chickens before any other bird because The Living Library was started many years ago by a wise chicken to save the world from destruction resulting from the Evils of Mankind.

Pearl's favorite Songbirds were The Wrens. These Pages of The Living Library visited with her throughout the day. She would start seeking answers from them. If they didn't know, they would help her get in touch with another Page of The Living Library who *could* help her.

Chapter 4

Pearl met with the wrens in The Backyard Garden as usual and described to them what she had seen.

The wrens were unsure what it might have been, but advised her that they would get her story of the sighting to The Raven With

Blue Eyes since her eyes could see what others could not. With her special sight and many travel experiences far beyond The Backyard Garden, she would have the best advice to help Pearl's search for the truth about The Curious Being.

Chapter 5

After covering as much territory as possible, The Raven With Blue Eyes decided to return to The Backyard Garden. Then, a sudden storm made her river crossing more difficult than expected, but The Raven With Blue Eyes wouldn't give up. She had to report her findings to Pearl. She had made a solemn promise to help chickens before any other birds.

The Raven's persistence was inspiring to everyone whose life she touched, especially to those in The Kingdom of Birds who knew her best. That is the power of a solemn promise made with love.

Chapter 6

Like waiting for the tastiest fruit to ripen, Pearl waited for the answers that she needed. Somehow, Pearl sensed that those answers would be worth the wait just like fresh blueberries while helping her to learn about patience which she also needed.

The Raven With Blue Eyes had always set the standard for what was expected from any member of The Living Library. As soon as she landed in the Backyard Garden, she began to explain in the most organized way all that she had discovered during her travels.

Chapter 7

The Raven With Blue Eyes began by saying, "I know that you chickens in The Backyard Garden have often wondered about guardian angels that people have. You know that guardian angels are real because Jesus spoke about them in The Ancient Words.

You know he wouldn't talk about something that was not true. He said that little children have guardian angels watching over them and that those guardian angels behold their Father in Heaven.

As chickens, you have had Ravens like myself and our relatives, the Crows, to defend you in the world that you can see. But you need to know that you have other defenders in the world that you can't see. These are The Angels assigned to animals God has created rather than to people. And since you have glimpsed them with your own eyes, Pearl, your eyes must have a gift similar to my own Blue Eyes.

"Like all crows, I had blue eyes when I hatched. Our crow eyes normally turn brown as we grow older, but both my heart and my eyes stayed young."

Chapter 8

The Raven said, "Pearl, you are a chicken, and when The Great Gardener created chickens, the Angels all admired them even more than they admired Ravens with eyes like mine. Look carefully for what makes YOU special. That's one of the best things you can do.

The Angels must surely have been amazed that a creation with wings like their own angelic wings would be unable to fly very far or hardly at all, but surely you chickens have gifts from The Great Gardener that no other birds have, not even ravens like myself.

"Pearl, I think your heart must have also remained young, so perhaps that is why you can see what the other chickens can't see. You see a special beauty that only a young heart can see. It is a beauty that comes from the Eternal World of God, Our Great Gardener's Son."

Chapter 9

The Raven hoped to comfort Pearl with thoughts of the past. Seeing a Celestial Being here in the Terrestrial World can be quite frightening and was likely why angels always tell people, "Fear not" whenever they appear to them with a message.

"Your sister, Blanche, was the first of the chickens to be buried under the camellias here in The Backyard Garden. Because all of you chickens cared about her, all of you were concerned that she would not have someone to watch over her."

Pearl nodded her head in agreement, but her sorrow kept her from speaking, so the Raven continued.

"Your Backyard Gardener, was especially worried when he was not home, and he never wanted this house with its Backyard Garden that his grandparents had given him to be sold or for any of you to become homeless. He never wanted you chickens who lived in it to be hurt, and so he prayed and prayed again.

"Dear Pearl, you must understand and believe that whatever concerns the heart of a person concerns the heart of Jesus too," said The Raven With Blue Eyes. The heart of Jesus is the first beating heart of flesh to ever enter The Kingdom of Heaven."

Chapter 10

The Raven continued, "Not only are there angels who watch over particular kinds of animals like dogs and cats, there are also angels who watch over animals with particular conditions, such as being lame and unable to walk.

Some animals are born with a missing or misshaped limb. Others lose a limb through an accident. Being able to move is essential, so being lame is a real challenge for some animals.

"The upraised arm of an angel can support and steady the lame animal since all animals are precious in the sight of Jesus who the Angels obey.

"But that is all that the hands of angels can do. If they had hands like people, they could do more.

"Jesus is particularly concerned about those animals who understand The Language of the Heart. This is the special language of God's own heart that people can also understand. It lets people communicate with animals like kittens and calves or pups and cubs and even chickens."

Chapter 11

As The Raven continued, Pearl learned that some angels help the forgotten animals. They are the ones who have been tied up and ignored or placed into cages and forced to perform tricks to entertain people. Others have been dumped in an abandoned spot where they have no one to rescue them and take care for them.

Our own ginger cat named Ernest was just such a pet once. Someone had dumped him at the end of our dead-end street near where The Big Boy at the End of The Street lives.

Pearl continued telling me all that she had learned from The Raven With Blue Eyes, and I am recording all of this so you can learn from Pearl.

Pearl said, "We chickens are grateful for the angel who led Ernest to our Backyard Garden where he protects our food from field mice. It seems clear that Ernest wants nothing more than to be fed and loved and to know that he is helping others who are loved by Jesus.

"And now that I am the only chicken left here in The Backyard Garden, I am more grateful than ever before to have him here."

Chapter 12

Pearl continued teaching me, "Any angel who has been given the task of tending to the hurt animals is particularly sorrowful over the hurt pets.

"They are saddened because people have hands through which the comfort and healing of

God can flow to those pets. The hands of angels are unable to do this work when tending to the hurt ones.

"The Great Gardener himself told The First Man and The First Woman to take care of and have dominion over the animals that He had created.

"He never tells people to do something without giving them the ability to do it. If only people would believe that their hands, this world would be such a very different place!"

Chapter 13

With so many friends who are songbird Pages in The Living Library, Pearl was happy to learn that there were angels who were assigned to look after the songbirds of The Living Library since even God's helpers can need help.

These special angels use copies of The Ancient Words in The Language of The Songbirds to ensure that their songs correctly use The Language of the Heart, the only language directly from God Himself and understood by whosoever has ears to hear and a heart to worship.

Chapter 14

Usually, Pearl and the other chickens felt safe in their Backyard Garden Home. Part of this was because the Raven with Blue Eyes and Her Squadron of Crows kept watch over them from high in the pine trees, but when they were off on a mission elsewhere, there was always an angel to watch for any activity by The Absence of Love who opposed God and all God created with His awesome Love. This angel could call on dozens more with weapons to defend the chickens of The Backyard Garden.

Hearing this, Pearl realized that she never needed to allow any fear into her heart. Fear and doubt might try to pass themselves off as friends, but they would never be her friends if sent by The Absence of Love.

Chapter 15

The Raven With Blue Eyes had seen how Pearl and the other chickens had come to believe that they are able to make their way through every challenge they encountered including Tuxedo Cats and Sewer Rats, but they needed more than believing in themselves.

Much of their success had to do with An Angel of Surmounting Challenges assigned to them by The Great Gardener. This angel taught them to trust only in The Great Gardener Himself, The One Who Never Changes and is therefore completely reliable.

Chapter 16

My chickens relied on the help of An Angel of Expectant Vision quite often. This Angel helped them to see ahead and predict what would likely happen in the future based on what had happened in the past.

Often, Pearl and the other chickens learned from the mistakes that they made, just as people do.

If there was ever a message from The Great Gardener for them about what would be their best choice, then An Angel of Expectant Vision would be the one to deliver it to them after reminding them of their past lessons learned by experience.

Pearl had found it was best to listen for any message beginning with "Now is the time to..." and especially "Fear not..."

Chapter 17

The Angel of Radiant Beauty is the last angel that The Raven With Blue Eyes told Pearl about and that Pearl told me about.

There was no doubt in my mind that this kind of angel had shared God's Radiant Beauty with Pearl and all of the chickens and other animals that I have loved throughout the years.

It is likely that An Angel of Radiant Beauty has the easiest task of any of the angels who watch over chickens and other animals.

Chickens are always beautiful. It is a beauty that comes from within. They simply are beautiful because The Great Gardener made them that way and shared His Gracious Love with them. This is also true of all people.

Rather than bestowing beauty, this angel's only task is to open the eyes of those looking at an animal or a person. This angel helps them to more clearly see what God has already given to His Creation. Surely, beauty is experienced in the heart of the beholder, and if you have ever loved anyone, then you know this quite well.

As I often say, "Pearl, you are so beautiful. And I thank God for giving me the eyes and heart to appreciate the beauty with which He has blessed you."

Chapter 18

Pearl had learned some amazing lessons from seeing The Curious Being and discussing Angels with The Raven, but there were even more lessons that she knew simply from listening to Jesus with her heart the way we all should.

Pearl fully knew that The Great Gardener's Son is far above every single angel even if they were all combined into one enormous angel, should that even be possible.

Now that He has returned to His Father in Heaven after living among us and being clothed in flesh like our own, his abilities have been spread out to others like his angels and his people.

To Pearl, it seems we are all still living in Day Six from "The Book of Beginnings." We have not fully arrived at Day Seven, The Day of Rest, because God is still creating - only now He is creating goodness through our hearts and hands, and that is his call to us.

Soon Jesus will return and usher in Day Seven, The Day of Rest for ALL. Then, The Garden of Angels will rejoice with everything that has breath, including chickens like Pearl!

Now It Is Your Turn!

❦

Pearl decided that our readers might appreciate a chance to do some art and illustration work of their own and also share their ideas about the angels in this book by using whatever colors and words they felt worked best.

Just remember what Pearl tells herself whenever she does anything creative:
"*There are no wrong colors and no wrong words.*"

Here are the first six of the angels found in this book. They are the ones that have do tasks that people can also do with their hands and hearts.

The Angel Who Defends All Animals

What types of predators might your favorite pet need to be defended from? What can you do with your heart and hands to make sure that your favorite pet stays safe?

The Angel Who Watches Over Pet Graves

What pet of your has died? Take some time to thank God for all the good times that particular pet brought into your life. Also thank God for sending his angels to watch over your pet's grave or ashes wherever they may be.

An Angel Admiring the Creation of Chickens

What special gift did God give to you when he created you?

An Angel Who
Tends the Lame Ones

Have you ever seen a lame animal? If you have, how did it make you feel? If you haven't, how do you imagine you would feel?

An Angel Who Helps
the Forgotten Ones

Have you ever seen an animal who appeared forgotten and uncared for? How did this make you feel? Did you want to do something to help the forgotten animal? If there was nothing that you could do, would this be a situation where you would want to tell an adult?

An Angel Who Helps
the Hurt Ones

How do you feel when you see an animal who is hurt? Do you try to help it? Do you feel cautious about it being afraid and hurting you even though you might try to help it? When might this be an example of when you would need to let an adult know? When helping might not be safe for you, can kind words and a prayer to God help?

God Is Still Creating Through the Hearts and Hands of His People

With your own heart and hands as someone who loves and listens to God, what can you do to create goodness for the people and animals around you?

About The Author and Illustrator

John Spiers is a writer, artist, and guardian to a small flock of chickens who live in the center of his backyard garden in Coastal Virginia.

While he often produced small writing and drawing projects, he never found his creative purpose until he decided to raise some baby chicks who became the characters in his stories and the subjects of his drawings. His work seeks to share the same joy that he feels when spending time with his flock of backyard chickens, and he happily includes bits of "chicken wisdom" about life he has learned from them.

With only Pearl remaining from his original flock of six chickens, he and Pearl are creating new books about life in The Backyard Garden.

https: MyLifeWithGraciePress.com

Notes

Use these next pages to record your own
notes that you can turn into a delightful
story just like Pearl would do!

We Always Have Room for Another Friend
https://GraciePress.com